RAYMOND RABBIT'S EARLY MORNING

Lynne Dennis

M
MACMILLAN CHILDREN'S BOOKS

First published 1987 by
MACMILLAN CHILDREN'S BOOKS
A division of Macmillan Publishers Limited
London and Basingstoke
Associated companies throughout the world

British Library Cataloguing in Publication Data
Dennis, Lynne
    Raymond Rabbit's early morning.
    I. Title
    823'.914 [J]   PZ7

ISBN 0-333-43773-X

Typeset by Universe Typesetters Ltd

Printed and bound in Hong Kong

RAYMOND RABBIT'S
EARLY MORNING

Raymond Rabbit woke to
the warm friendly light of his
night lamp. He wasn't
sleepy any more, so he got
out of bed.

Raymond Rabbit tried on
lots of clothes. He liked his
blue velvet jacket best and
that was what he wore.

As he did every morning,
Raymond Rabbit brushed
his teeth, then cleaned his
face and paws. Even though
there was no one there to
see what he had done, he
did a very good job.

Remembering what to do next in the morning wasn't easy. Raymond Rabbit even forgot that playtime always comes *after* breakfast.

So down the stairs he went.
"I could eat some breakfast now,"
Raymond said to himself.

On the way to the kitchen,
Raymond Rabbit tried to
phone his friend to ask him
to come and play.

Choosing what to have for
breakfast was fun. He chose
something for everyone
in the family and lettuce
jam for himself.

Raymond Rabbit knew his
mother enjoyed listening to
the radio during breakfast.
He was just tall enough to
switch it on by himself.

Raymond Rabbit began
eating without waiting for the
others. Then the voice on the
radio said, "It's much too early
to be up, so listen to our
music from your cosy bed."
And he really *did* feel sleepy.

On his way back to bed,
Raymond Rabbit peeped
into his parents' room.
They were fast asleep.

Raymond crept into bed
with his parents. When they
woke up, he'd tell them all
about how he had started
the day. In the meantime,
he'd just close his eyes . . . .